Du Iz Tak?

Carson Ellis

WALKER BOOKS
AND SUBSIDIARIES
LONDON • BOSTON • SYDNEY • AUCKLAND

Du iz tak?

Ma nazoot.

Ta ta!

Du iz tak?
Ma ebadow unk plonk.
Du kimma plonk?
Ma nazoot.

Ru badda unk ribble.
Su.
Bore inkin Icky.

Icky!
Icky!
ICKY!

Icky, ru badda unk ribble.

Unk ribble!

Su!
Ru daddin doodin unk furt!
Su!

RUP FURT!

VOOBECK!
BOOBY VOOBECK!
Rup furt.

Su!

Du iz tak?
Oooooh.
Ho Ooky!

Unk gladdenboot!
Iz unk gladdenboot!
Unk gladdenboot!
Unk scrivadelly gladdenboot!
Ahhhh.
Unk gladdenboot!
Su!

Iz tak unk
gladdenboot?
Unk gladdenboot!

Ta ta, oodas!

Ta ta, Icky.
Ta ta, Ooky.

Ta ta, furt.

Du iz tak?

For the good folks of the KBK

First published 2016 by Walker Books Ltd
87 Vauxhall Walk, London SE11 5HJ

This edition published 2017

2 4 6 8 10 9 7 5 3

This book has been typeset in Bauer Bodoni

Printed in China

British Library Cataloguing in Publication Data: a catalogue record for this book is available from the British Library

ISBN 978-1-4063-7343-1

www.walker.co.uk